S0-BDO-347

ADAM SHARP

The Spy Who Barked

by George Edward Stanley
illustrated by Guy Francis

A STEPPING STONE BOOK™
Random House New York

To my mother, with love. You didn't laugh when I told you I wanted to be a spy.
—G.E.S.

To my mom and dad
—G.F.

 Published in the United States by Random House Children's Books, a division of Random House, Inc., New York, and simultaneously in Canada by Random House of Canada Limited, Toronto. Originally published by Golden Books, an imprint of Random House Children's Books, a division of Random House, Inc., New York, in 2002.

www.randomhouse.com/kids

Library of Congress Cataloging-in-Publication Data
Stanley, George Edward.
Adam Sharp : the spy who barked / by George Edward Stanley ;
illustrated by Guy Francis.
p. cm.
"A Stepping Stone book."
SUMMARY: Eight-year-old spy Adam Sharp pursues the very short Ambassador of Barkastan, who has stolen a top-secret computer program, DOGBARK, that will let him understand the language of dogs.
ISBN 0-307-26412-2 (pbk.) — ISBN 0-307-46412-1 (lib. bdg.)
[1. Spies—Fiction. 2. Dogs—Fiction.] I. Francis, Guy, ill. II. Title.
PZ7.S78694Af 2003 [Fic]—dc21 2002013419

First Random House Edition
Printed in the United States of America 11 10 9 8 7 6 5 4 3 2

Contents

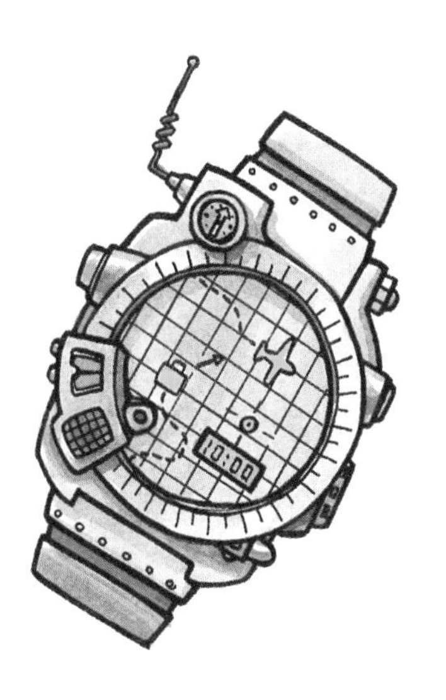

code
criminal
cold
covert

1
Secret Agent Kid

"Class! Class! Wake up!" Mrs. Digby said. "Please open your spelling books to page seven!"

Adam Sharp yawned. He was so sleepy. He'd stayed up too late last night practicing judo.

Adam opened his spelling book. But he knew he wouldn't be in class very long. A red light was blinking on the television monitor above Mrs. Digby's head. It meant that the janitor would come by to get him in a few minutes.

That's because Adam Sharp wasn't just a student. He was also a secret agent for IM-8. IM-8 agents were assigned the secret missions that other agents were too scared to go on.

There was a knock at the door. The janitor stuck his head in the room. "The Gifted and Talented Teacher needs to see Adam Sharp," he said.

"Of course!" Mrs. Digby turned to Adam. "We're so proud of you," she said. "You're so gifted and talented. And well dressed, too!"

"Thank you," Adam said. He buttoned the jacket of his tuxedo and straightened his black tie.

Adam was the only student at Friendly Elementary School in the Gifted and Talented Program. But there was a good reason for that.

Suddenly, Jurgen Slug stood up. Jurgen had only been at Friendly Elementary School for a week, but Adam didn't like him. He thought Jurgen was mean and selfish. Jurgen also smelled kind of funny. Adam

always felt sleepy when he was around.

"I'm gifted and talented, too, Mrs. Digby," Jurgen said. "Why can't I go?"

Adam was surprised. No one had ever asked that question before.

"You have to be chosen by the Gifted and Talented Teacher, Jurgen," Mrs. Digby said. "You weren't chosen."

Adam followed the janitor out of the room. The janitor wasn't really a janitor. He was J. He made the gadgets that Adam used for spying.

They walked down the hallway to the janitor's closet and went inside. J closed the door. Then he pushed a red button and another door opened in front of them. It led to a big room full of big computers. This was the headquarters of IM-8.

The Gifted and Talented Teacher sat behind a big desk. But he wasn't really a teacher. He was T. T was the head of IM-8.

"Good morning, Sharp," T said to Adam. "I need to hear your report on DOGBARK. What do you think of it?"

"It's a great computer program, sir. The world needs it," Adam said. "No one has ever known before what dogs were saying. It's time we did."

T nodded. "I agree. That's why I've arranged for you to address the United Nations next week."

"I'll be ready, sir," Adam said.

Adam went back to his classroom. No one was there. He checked his watch. It was time for recess. Good. Adam liked recess.

Then Adam saw something bad. His lunchbox was missing! The lunchbox wasn't just a lunchbox. It had a secret compartment with a laptop computer. Someone had stolen DOGBARK!

Adam raced down the hall. Just as he got to the janitor's closet, J opened the door. Adam stepped inside.

“What’s the problem?” T asked.

“My lunchbox was under my desk,” Adam said. “Somebody stole it!”

“Kids don’t steal lunchboxes,” J said. “That’s why I put a secret compartment in yours. I thought it would be safe.”

Adam thought for a minute. “That means I’m not the only spy in Mrs. Digby’s class!” he said. He turned to T. “I need to go to recess!”

“It’s no time for playing, Sharp!” T said. “You have to find DOGBARK!”

“That’s what I plan to do,” Adam said grimly.

He hurried out to the playground

and counted his classmates. Just as he suspected. Someone was missing! Jurgen Slug!

Adam pushed a blue button on his watch. It turned on a homing device inside his lunchbox. A road map of Friendly, Maryland, appeared. It had a moving yellow square on it.

That's strange, Adam thought. His lunchbox was headed toward Friendly Airport!

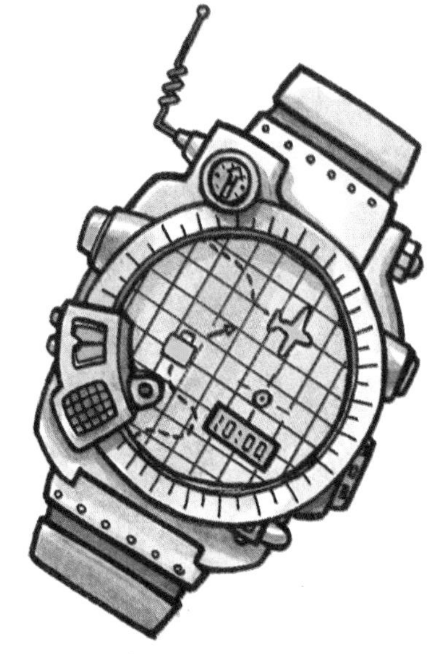

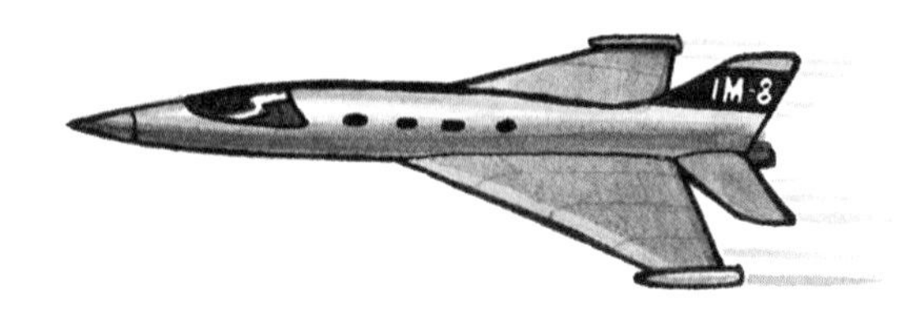

2
The Very Short Ambassador

T told the principal that Adam was going on a Gifted and Talented field trip. That really meant Adam was going on an IM-8 mission.

Adam raced home on his bicycle.

His mother and father were in the living room. His mother was reading the newspaper. His father was reading a romance novel. It was one that Adam's mother had written.

"Mom! Dad! I won't be home for supper," Adam shouted as he raced up the stairs to his room. "I'm going on a Gifted and Talented field trip."

"Oh, that's wonderful, Adam!" his mother called. "I'm so glad you're in the Gifted and Talented Program."

"These trips are very educational, son," his father added. "They'll help you get into college."

Adam unlocked the door to his room. Inside, it looked like IM-8 Headquarters. Only smaller. Adam's parents never went in his room. But it was an IM-8 rule that he keep his door locked. And Adam followed the rules.

Adam grabbed his overnight bag. He always kept it packed. He ran back downstairs. He jumped onto his bicycle and raced to the airport.

Adam leaned his bicycle against the airplane hangar. He ran out to the IM-8 plane and climbed aboard. "Hi, T!" he said. "Where are we headed?"

"Holland," T told him. "Jurgen Slug's plane just took off."

"Who's our contact there?" Adam asked.

"Tulip Belle," T replied.

Adam punched a key on the plane's computer. Tulip's file appeared on the screen. She was eight years old, too. She went to Vriendelijk Elementary School in Amsterdam.

Adam punched another key on the computer. The speaker crackled, and then a voice said, "*Ja?*"

"*Goedendag*, Tulip," Adam said in Dutch.

"Hello, Adam. What's up?" Tulip said in English.

Adam told Tulip about Jurgen Slug and the missing lunchbox.

"I'll leave for the airport at once," Tulip said. "But you need to hurry. We're having the worst snowstorm in a hundred years. The airport may close at any minute."

Adam shivered. This was going to be a cold assignment. Good thing he'd brought his mittens.

Adam and T followed Jurgen Slug's

plane across the Atlantic Ocean to Amsterdam. Minutes after they landed, the airport closed.

"There's Jurgen Slug's plane," T said. He pointed across the snow-covered runway. A big black car was parked beside the plane. Jurgen Slug climbed in, and the car pulled away.

"That car had General Menace's logo on it!" Adam said. He clenched his fists. General Menace was Adam's archenemy.

"This doesn't look good," T said.

Just then, another big black car pulled up. A girl got out. She had on a

Dutch cap and wooden shoes.

"That must be Tulip!" Adam cried. He grabbed his overnight bag. "See you later, T. I'll be in touch."

Adam hurried to meet Tulip. "Wow! I didn't know Dutch girls really wore wooden shoes," he said.

"We don't," Tulip said. "We were

having a play at school when you contacted me."

"Oh!" Adam said. "Sorry!"

"That's okay," Tulip said.

Adam and Tulip got into the big black car. The driver took off through the heavy snow.

"Jurgen Slug is not Jurgen Slug," Tulip reported. "He's the very short Ambassador to the Republic of Barkastan."

"Barkastan! Of course! They have more dogs than people!" Adam said. "But how does the Ambassador plan to use DOGBARK? And why is General

Menace helping him? That's what we have to find out." Adam looked at Tulip. "Where are we headed?" he asked.

"The Amsterdam train station. It's the only way out of the country now,"

she said. "General Menace's driver bought the Ambassador a ticket to Istanbul before he picked him up at the airport."

"Istanbul! Of course!" Adam said. "Istanbul is in Turkey, and Turkey has a border with Barkastan. That's where the Ambassador is going! We have to get my lunchbox back."

Tulip looked at her watch. "Hurry!" she shouted to the driver. "The train leaves in five minutes!"

3

Nighty-Night!

The Turkey Express was just pulling out of the station. Adam and Tulip ran down the platform and jumped aboard.

"Whew!" Adam said. "We made it!"

"*Ja*," Tulip said.

The conductor looked at Adam's tuxedo. "I'm sorry, sir. We have no room in first class," he said.

Adam was disappointed. An IM-8 agent always traveled first class. But second class would have to do. He fixed his bow tie. "Okay," he said. The conductor handed them their tickets.

"We're looking for a really short man," Adam said to the conductor. "Is there one on this train?"

The conductor thought for a minute. "There are twenty really short men on the train," he replied.

"Too bad," Adam said. "It may take us a while to find the Ambassador."

"*Ja*," Tulip said.

The conductor showed them to a

second-class car. They sat down. Two really short men were sitting across from them. But neither one looked like Jurgen Slug.

"I have an idea!" Tulip said. She whispered it to Adam.

"That's a great idea," Adam said.

They left their seats and walked

through the train, holding newspapers in front of their faces. But instead of reading, both of them started to bark. They barked for several minutes. No one paid much attention.

Finally, they reached the last car on the train. "The Ambassador has to be in one of these rooms," Adam said.

"*Ja*," Tulip said.

They started barking again.

Suddenly, a really short man opened a door. It was the Ambassador. "You!" he gasped.

"Yes!" Adam said. He and Tulip rushed into the Ambassador's room. "We knew you'd try DOGBARK if you heard barking dogs. We were right."

Adam sniffed the air. He yawned. Tulip yawned, too. All of a sudden, Adam felt tired. He wanted to grab the lunchbox. But his arms wouldn't move.

"I can't keep my eyes open!" Adam said to Tulip.

“Me, either,” Tulip said.

“How do you like my aftershave lotion?” the Ambassador said. “It’s called ‘Nighty-Night’!”

“So that’s why I kept feeling sleepy in Mrs. Digby’s class!” Adam cried.

With that, he and Tulip fell sound asleep.

4

Up and Adam

Adam opened his eyes. The train was stopped. Tulip was asleep on the floor next to him. The door was open. The Ambassador was gone.

Adam checked his watch. They had been asleep for a long time. He looked out the window. All he saw was snow.

Then the conductor ran by the door.

Adam stopped him. "Are we in Istanbul yet?" he asked.

"Almost. But we can't go any farther," the conductor replied. "There's too much snow."

Just then, Adam heard a loud noise outside. He lowered the window and stuck out his head. There were two snowmobiles beside the train.

"Tulip!" Adam shouted. "Wake up!"

Like all IM-8 agents, Tulip was trained to wake up quickly. "What's wrong?" she asked.

"Look! It's the Ambassador!" Adam said. "He and another evil person are escaping on snowmobiles!"

Tulip and Adam ran to the end of the train car. They opened the door and jumped out.

"Watch this!" Tulip said.

She threw her wooden shoe at the Ambassador. The Ambassador ducked. The shoe hit the other evil person in the head. He fell off the snowmobile.

"Good job, Tulip!" Adam said. "Come on!"

Tulip ran and picked up her wooden shoe. Then she and Adam jumped on the snowmobile. Adam put it in gear. They roared off after the Ambassador.

They raced through the snowy streets of Istanbul. They raced over the Ataturk Bridge.

"He's headed for the mountains!" Adam shouted. "That's the border with Barkastan!"

"We have to stop him before he gets there," Tulip said. "We don't want to cross the border."

Adam shuddered. Tulip was right. Very few people went to Barkastan. It had the meanest dogs in the world.

The snow was getting heavier.

"I wish we could stop and make a snowman, don't you?" Adam yelled.

"*Ja*," Tulip sighed.

It started to get dark. Adam turned on his headlights. The Ambassador did the same.

They rode through the night.

From time to time, Adam pushed a red button on his watch. The watch sent a message to a satellite. The satellite told T where they were.

When the sun came up, Adam saw the mountains.

"The top of that mountain is the Barkastan border!" Tulip said.

They had gained on the Ambassador during the night. Now he was only a few yards in front of them.

Suddenly, Adam heard a noise. It sounded like a thousand barking dogs. "Do you hear that?" he asked.

"The dogs of Barkastan!" Tulip gasped. "Now we'll never get your lunchbox back!"

5
The Dogs of Barkastan

The dogs of Barkastan appeared at the top of the mountain. They all stopped at once.

"They're waiting to welcome the Ambassador back home!" Tulip said.

"No! No! Look, Tulip! That's not what they're doing," Adam shouted. "They're growling! They're showing their teeth. They look like they want to bite the Ambassador."

"That's strange," Tulip said. "Why won't they let him into Barkastan?"

"That's what we need to find out!" Adam shouted. "Hold on!"

The snowmobile shot forward. It headed straight for the Ambassador. The Ambassador saw them coming. He started down the mountain toward them.

"We're going to crash!" Tulip yelled.

But Adam turned left. And the Ambassador turned right. They chased each other round and round.

All of a sudden, the Ambassador's snowmobile sputtered. So did Adam and Tulip's. They looked at each other.

"Are you out of gas?" shouted the Ambassador.

"Yes!" shouted Adam. He pushed the red button on his watch.

"Me, too," shouted the Ambassador. He held up the lunchbox. "But you'll never get this back!" he cried.

In the distance, the dogs of Barkastan continued to bark. But now they were barking in English. "Help us! Help us!" they barked. "The people of Barkastan are mean!"

"The Ambassador turned on the computer by mistake!" Adam said. "It's translating what the dogs of Barkastan are barking. They aren't evil after all."

Adam looked at the Ambassador. "Now I know why you stole my lunchbox!" he shouted. "You didn't want the world to know what the dogs of Barkastan were saying!"

"That's right!" the Ambassador shouted back. "They're our dogs. We can treat them any way we want. It's none of the world's business."

"That's what he thinks!" Adam said to Tulip. He heard another snowmobile pull up.

"It's General Menace!" Tulip cried.

"Well, well, well," General Menace said when he reached them. "Adam Sharp and Tulip Belle. Heh! Heh! Heh!"

"What's your stake in this, General Menace?" Adam asked. "Why do you want DOGBARK?"

"My spies tell me that the world is going to the dogs," General Menace said. "So if I can find out what the dogs are saying, I can rule the world! Heh! Heh! Heh!"

Adam shivered. *What a horrible thought!* he thought.

"Toss me the lunchbox!" General Menace shouted to the Ambassador. "The dogs won't let you back into Barkastan. You don't need it now."

Just then, Adam heard a whirring noise. He knew exactly what it was.

"Get ready, Tulip," Adam whispered. "When the Ambassador tosses the lunchbox, throw your shoe at it!"

The whirring noise got louder.

"Toss the lunchbox!" screamed General Menace. "Toss the lunchbox!"

Suddenly, a helicopter appeared in

the sky. Its blades whipped up the snow. Adam felt like he was in a blizzard.

"Toss it!" General Menace screamed again. "Toss it!" The Ambassador tossed the lunchbox.

"He's got a good arm," Adam said. "He should play professional baseball."

"*Ja*," Tulip said. "He'll need a new job."

Adam watched the lunchbox soar over them. "Now!" he shouted.

Tulip threw the wooden shoe.

"You've got a good arm, too, Tulip!" Adam said.

The shoe hit the lunchbox. The

lunchbox fell into Adam's hands. The shoe fell by Tulip's feet.

General Menace screamed. He roared toward them on his snowmobile.

Just then, a rope dropped down from the helicopter. Adam grabbed it with one hand. Tulip put on her shoe and grabbed Adam. T pulled them up into his helicopter.

General Menace waved a fist in the air. "I'll get you, Adam Sharp!" he shouted.

The next day, Adam was back at school. Several kids asked Mrs. Digby

IM-8

where Jurgen Slug was. She said she thought he had gone to another school.

Adam didn't say anything. IM-8 agents never talked about missions. Even to teachers.

During math, J opened the door to his classroom. "The Gifted and Talented Teacher needs Adam Sharp," he said.

"Of course." Mrs. Digby smiled at Adam. "We're so proud of you. You're so gifted and talented."

Adam followed J to the janitor's closet. They went inside.

"I've read your report, Sharp," T said. "Good job!"

"It's not over yet, sir," Adam said. "Next week, I talk to the United Nations. We're going to help the dogs of Barkastan."

T nodded. "That's what we're here for."

Adam left IM-8 Headquarters. He went back to his classroom. It was almost time for recess. There was a new slide on the playground. He could hardly wait to try it out.